sparkle town fairies

Susie
the
Sapphire
Fairy
and the Glitter Games

Sarah Creese ✳ Lara Ede

make
believe
ideas

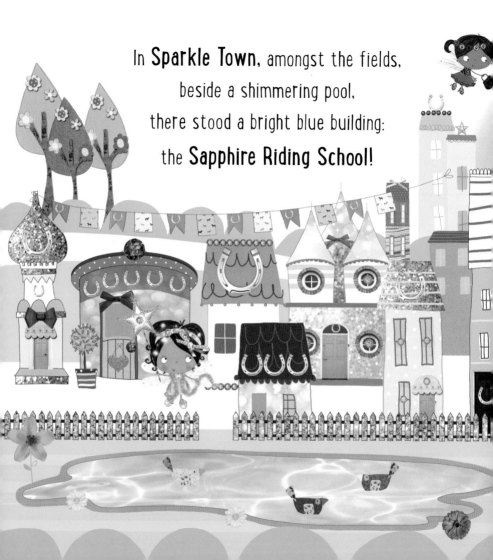

In **Sparkle Town**, amongst the fields,
beside a shimmering pool,
there stood a bright blue building:
the **Sapphire Riding School!**

RIDING 🐴 SCHOOL

The **school** was home to horses
with gleaming, spiral horns
in every **rainbow** shade – they were...

the **Sparkle Town UNICORNS!**

Susie the Sapphire Fairy
took charge of sports and games.

She cared for all the unicorns
and knew each one by name.

With her glittering, **sapphire wand,**
Susie would invent

sparkling balls,

Whooooosh

and **nets**

and **sticks**

Swish
Swish

Whizzzzz

for **any** sports event!

Susie **loved** all kinds of sports,
but best of all, by far,
was Fairy Land's great **Glitter Games** –
creator of **SUPERSTARS**.

SPARKLE TOWN
PRESENTS

Sparkle Town was this year's host,
so Susie **HAD** to win.
She said, "I'm sure we'll beat them all.
Let training time begin!"

THE GLITTER GAMES

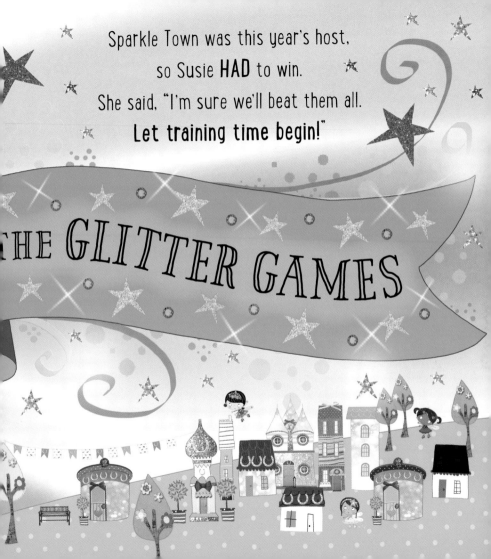

Not like that, like this!

The fairies trained hard every day,
and Susie took the **lead**.
"Not like that, like this!" she groaned.
"Now try again — with **SPEED!**"

This is hard work.

This went on for hours and hours
'til Daphne said, "Let's rest."
But Susie cried, "No time to stop —
we have to be the best!"

Can't we rest now?

Fed up with being told what to do
and Susie's tough regime,

the fairies said, "We've had enough!
We want you **OFF** the team."

SUSIE FUMED! Her cheeks turned red.
She stomped off with a **HUMPH**
and wouldn't talk to anyone —
she truly had the **grumps**.

Good job, Team!

With **Susie gone,**
the team trained on
through rain
and windy weather.
And Susie saw that
without her...
they worked better
together.

Hmm, maybe
I was wrong.

At last the **GLITTER GAMES** began!
The fairies were prepared.

Over here!

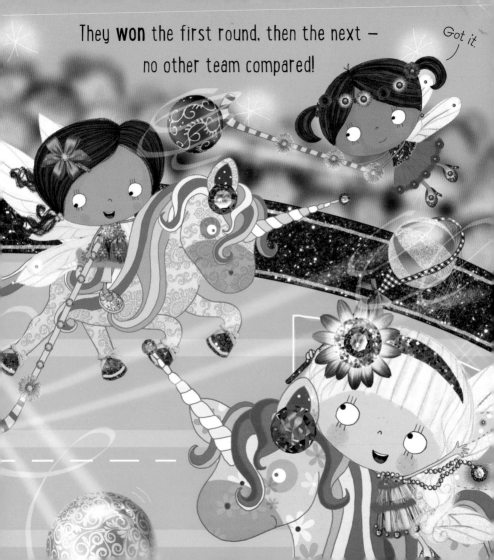

They **won** the first round, then the next —
no other team compared!

Got it.

They made it to the **final match,**
and here, their biggest threat:

Team Glitter
is the best!

the **Glitter City fairy team —**
their toughest rivals yet.

The fairies tried; they **whizzed** and **charged**
but couldn't get ahead.

The Glitters
are too good!

At half-time they felt tired and down.
"We're losing!" Rosie said.

And then **DISASTER** truly struck when Daphne **tripped** and fell!

"**Time out!**" shouted the referee.

"**Team Talk!**" Rosie yelled.

ot so sparkly now, are we.

Meanwhile, Susie **watched**, wide-eyed, and despite how cross she felt, seeing her friends in trouble just made her want to **help**.

In a flash, she flew to them and said, "You **can't** give in!
You each have special skills and strengths. There's still a chance to wi

"Rosie, you're good in defence; the rest of you, attack!
I could fill in Daphne's place — if you'll have me back."

They nodded and smiled at Susie:
"Let's give this plan a try!"
With Susie by their side again,
they **flew** into the sky.

The fairies tried their very best:
they listened and worked as one.
But the **Glitters** were still better,
and in the end... **THEY** won.

SPARKLE TOWN	GLITTER CITY
11	14

WINNER ★ GLITTER CITY ★ WINNER

Susie **frowned**. "I let you down.
I know now I was mean
when I didn't listen in training
or work well with the team.
You're better off **without me**."
She looked down at her feet...

Back at the school. Susie said, "We don't need to feel blue.
Let's be **proud** of second place — that's still special, too."

Susie learnt that friends come **first**; they share the lows and highs
And **friendship**, not the Glitter Games, was her very greatest **priz**